WHAT'S A GHOST GOING TO DO?

by JANE THAYER

PICTURES BY SEYMOUR FLEISHMAN

A WORLD'S WORK CHILDREN'S BOOK

Also by Jane Thayer
and Seymour Fleishman

Gus and the Baby Ghost
Gus was a Christmas Ghost
Gus was a Friendly Ghost
Gus was a Mexican Ghost
I'm Not a Cat, said Emerald
A Little Dog Called Kitty
Quiet on Account of Dinosaur

Text copyright © 1966 by Catherine Woolley
Illustrations copyright © 1966 by Seymour Fleishman
All rights reserved
First published in Great Britain 1972 by
World's Work Ltd
The Windmill Press, Kingswood, Tadworth, Surrey
Third impression 1979

Printed and bound at William Clowes & Sons Limited
Beccles and London
SBN 437 79408 3

Gus was a friendly ghost,
who lived in an attic flat
in an old house in the country.
The house was so old
that its shingles curled,
its windows were cracked,
and its paint was peeling.

In the summer Mr. and Mrs. Scott
and Susie and Sammy Scott
lived in the house.
The Scotts didn't believe in ghosts,
but when Gus banged and clanked
with his bang-clank equipment,
they told their friends proudly,
"We've got a ghost named Gus."
When the Scotts moved out in the autumn,
Mouse moved in.
Gus made cheesecake for him,
and they played draughts
by a crackling log fire.
Summer and winter, Gus led a happy life.

One day, when the birds had flown south
and the Scotts would be leaving soon,
Gus was hovering about
when he heard Mr. Scott
talking to Mrs. Scott.
"I think I'll sell the house
to the government," Mr. Scott said.
"The government is buying old houses
and knocking them down
to make a park here.
They will knock this one down."
"Then we can build a new house,"
Mrs. Scott said.

Gus was shocked. Knock the house down?
It was the only home he had ever known.
Where would he go if they tore it down?
Oh, I've got to put some thoughts
in Mr. Scott's head, he decided.
He followed Mr. Scott round the house,
trying to put some thoughts in his head.
"This is a lovely old house!"
cried Gus in ghostly language.
Mr. Scott wasn't listening.

He followed Mr. Scott round the garden.
"There aren't many like it left!"
cried Gus in ghostly language.
Mr. Scott wasn't listening.
"Don't sell it!" begged Gus.
Still Mr. Scott didn't hear.
Gus climbed back to his attic flat,
groaning with despair.
He couldn't go with the Scotts.
Ghosts never live in *new* houses.
What was he going to do?

The Scotts sold the house.
They began to clear everything out.
They held a sale,
and people came to buy
the furniture and dishes.

Gus wandered about
as things were carried out,
wailing and wringing his hands.

The house was empty now.
The Scotts closed the door
for the last time.
"Good-bye, house," they said rather sadly.
"Good-bye, Gus."
"Don't go!" cried Gus in anguish
from the window of his attic flat.
But the Scotts went off.
Gus waved his handkerchief,
ghostly tears streaming down,
until the car was lost from sight.

The house was empty now, except for Gus.

He was very lonely.

Besides, the house might

be knocked down any minute.

Down the road stood an even older house.

Gus knew the old ghost,

named Captain Obadiah Paine,

who lived there.

In a creeping, curling, ghost-like fog

he floated down the road.

"I am going to lose my home,"
he told the old ghost
Captain Obadiah Paine.
"Would it be possible to rent a room here?
I would help
with the banging
and clanking."

The old ghost Captain Obadiah Paine
moaned and made other ghostly sounds.
"As a matter of fact," he groaned
in his ghostly manner,
"this banging and clanking
is becoming too much for me.
If you will take over the job
you may move in."
"Oh, thank you, thank you!" cried Gus.
"Oh, I'll go and get my bang-clank equipment!"
He brought his bang-clank equipment
and moved into the attic
of the ancient house.
He was so grateful
to that old ghost Captain Obadiah Paine
for taking him in that he resolved to do
the best bang-clank job in the world.

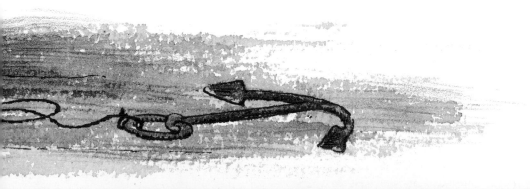

That night he banged and he clanked,
he clanked and he banged,
without a break.
He kept it up all night.
And the next night.
And the night after that.
At last the old ghost
Captain Obadiah Paine
came trembling upstairs.
"I am a nervous wreck from this racket!"
he shouted in his shaky old voice.
"Oh, excuse me!" exclaimed Gus.
"Oh, I'll bang very softly."

Captain Obadiah Paine
shook his ghostly old head.
"It's not going to work,
your living here.
I'm sorry. Good-bye."
Nothing Gus could say
would change that old ghost's mind.
Sorrowfully Gus gathered up
his bang-clank equipment.
In a creeping, curling, ghost-like fog
he floated up the road
to the lonely, empty old house
about to be torn down.

The next day Mouse came round.
"Shall I move in?" he inquired.
Gus shook his head.
"They're going to knock the house down.
Have you got some other place to go?"
"Oh, of course," said Mouse carelessly.
"A mouse can always find a house."
"May I go with you?" cried Gus.
"Oh, I suppose so,"
said Mouse indifferently.
"Come along."
Gus hastily gathered
his bang-clank equipment
and followed Mouse out.

Mouse led him to a hole
under the dry leaves in the woods.
Mouse dived into it.
Gus set down his bang-clank equipment
outside the door.
He began to squeeze through the hole.
Even though he was a ghostly ghost,
and held his breath,
it was a terribly tight fit.
Mouse popped impatiently out of another hole.
"Don't take all day," he said crossly.
"Help me!" gasped Gus.

Mouse popped into the hole again
and grabbed Gus's legs.
Gus wriggled, Mouse pulled,
and at last Gus found himself,
a little black and blue,
down in Mouse's house.

"There is not room for both of us,"
complained Mouse.
Gus made himself as small as he could.
He didn't want to be any bother.
But he soon saw,
from Mouse's muttering and stamping about,
that he was in the way.
He was quite uncomfortable, too,
in such cramped quarters.
In the night he heard rain
pounding on Mouse's house.

Oh, my bang-clank equipment will rust,
he thought in dismay!
"May I bring my bang-clank equipment
in out of the rain?" he asked.
"No, you may not," said Mouse.
Gus sat scrunched up
in a corner all night.
As soon as daylight came
he got up painfully
and wriggled his way back through the hole.
Sure enough,
his precious bang-clank equipment
was red with rust.
"Thanks just the same, Mouse,"
called Gus down the hole.
"I am going home.
I'll stay till they tear the house down."
He lugged his bang-clank equipment home
and spent the day removing the rust.

Once more he put his mind on
the problem of where to live.
I'll advertise, he thought.
He put an advertisement in the paper:

Ghost, named Gus,
experienced, friendly, needs a good home.

He looked in the letter-box every day,
but no reply came.
No one wanted to give a ghost a home.

Then a government man, Mr. McGovern,
came round to see if the house was empty,
so he could knock it down.
When Gus heard his key in the lock
he thought,
Oh, perhaps I have one last chance!
He hurried downstairs.
He followed
as Mr. McGovern walked from room to room.
"This is a lovely old house!"
cried Gus in loud ghostly language.
Mr. McGovern wasn't listening.
"There aren't many like it left!"
cried Gus in louder ghostly language.
Mr. McGovern wasn't listening.
"What's a ghost going to do?
Don't knock it down!" cried Gus,
and in his despair
he hammered Mr. McGovern on the head.

All Mr. McGovern seemed to feel
was a light breeze on his bald head.
But suddenly he stood still.
"I just had an idea!" he exclaimed.
Gus stood still too.
"This is a lovely old house.
There aren't many like it left,"
Mr. McGovern said.
Gus held his breath.
"I won't knock it down!"
cried Mr. McGovern.
"We'll use it for a museum
in the park!"
Gus fainted from joy.
The government man
got busy at once
on his wonderful idea.

He called in carpenters and painters.
They took off the old curling roof
and nailed on new shingles.
They repaired the window glass
and put on fresh white paint.
Gus was everywhere, he was so thrilled.

Mr. McGovern brought in
handsome old grandfather clocks,
spinning wheels, butter churns,
brass candlesticks,
and all sorts of antiques.
Gus ran his fingers lovingly
over the old things.
Mr. McGovern put up a sign, *Museum*.
He stood outside, admiring the place.
Gus stood behind him.
"That was a splendid idea of mine,"
Mr. McGovern said.

"All it needs is a ghost," said Gus.
"All it needs is a ghost,"
said Mr. McGovern.
"Where did I see
something about a ghost?
I know, in the paper."
He pulled the paper out of his pocket
and there was the advertisement:
Ghost, named Gus,
experienced, friendly, needs a good home.

"Answer it," said Gus,
who wanted to know he was welcome.
"I'll answer it," Mr. McGovern said.
He mailed a letter that said,
"Dear Gus, You are cordially invited
to make your home in the new Park Museum."
How will we know if he accepts?
Mr. McGovern wondered.
"Bang! Clank!" said Gus.
"Good!" said Mr. McGovern.

Then people poured in to see
all the antiques in the Park Museum.
Mr. McGovern explained
about hoopskirts and warming pans.
He told them to notice
the lovely old house,
for there weren't many like it left.

Gus looked after everything.
He banged and he clanked.
"And we've got a ghost!"
said Mr. McGovern proudly.